Signs and Symbols

Written by
Nigel Nelson

Illustrated by
Tony De Saulles

Thomson Learning
New York

Books in the series
Body Talk
Signs and Symbols

Picture acknowledgments

The publishers would like to thank the following for allowing their photographs to be reproduced in this book: Bruce Coleman Ltd., 5 (above/John Topham), 9 (below/Keith Gunnar); Chapel Studios 6 (John Heinrich), 10 (Zul); Eye Ubiquitous 7 (Davy Bold), 14 (below/Paul Thompson), 26 (Paul Seheult); the Hutchison Library 22, 27; Life File 24 (Graham Burns); Oxford Scientific Films Ltd., 8 (below/Mike Birkhead); Daniel Pangbourne 15, 16, 20, 21, 28, 29 (above); Photri 11; Tony Stone Worldwide 13 (above), 23, 25; ZEFA 4, 5 (below), 8 (above), 13 (below), 14 (above), 17, 18.

First published in the
United States in 1993 by
Thomson Learning
115 Fifth Avenue
New York, NY 10003

First published in 1993 by
Wayland (Publishers) Ltd.

Library of Congress Cataloging-in-Publication Data
Nelson, Nigel.
  Signs and symbols / written by Nigel Nelson : illustrations by Tony De Saulles.
      p.   cm. – (Nonverbal communications)
  Originally published: Hove, England : Wayland, 1993.
  Includes bibliographical references and index.
  ISBN 1-56847-100-9 : $12.95
  1. Signs and symbols – Juvenile literature. I De Saulles, Tony. II. Title.
III. Series.
P99.N45   1993
302.23 – dc20   93-27779

Printed in Italy

Contents

Words that are printed in **bold** are explained in the glossary.

Who needs words?

Signs and symbols are found all over the world. They give us information without using words. A good symbol is usually very simple. You can quickly guess what it means.

This symbol for **recycling** shows, without words, how these things can be used over and over again.

People who stay at this **campsite** may speak different languages, but the symbols can be understood by everyone. What might you find at this campsite?

Many signs tell you things that you need to know quickly. A no-smoking sign is a fast way to tell people that they may not smoke in a place.

Colors can help

The colors used in signs are often very important.

These faucet knobs do not say hot and cold on them, but you can tell which is which. The color red makes us think of words like hot, blood, or angry. This makes it a good color to use for danger or warning signs. Blue or green reminds us of water or cold things.

The red around this road sign is a warning. It warns drivers to be careful because children may be crossing the road.

Traffic lights use colors as signs: a red light means "stop." An amber light means "prepare to stop." A green light means "go."

On the road

Many road signs don't use words. Drivers must keep their eyes on the road, so symbols can quickly tell them what they need to know.

Road signs inside circles are often orders. What do you think these signs mean?

In Europe and some other places, signs inside a red triangle are warnings. What are drivers being warned about by these signs?

Activity

Draw your own set of warning signs such as, "Warning: broken glass" or "Danger: low-flying kites."

Some road signs, like this one from Florida, warn of possible dangers. What do you think might be found along this road?

NEXT 7 MILES

Shop signs

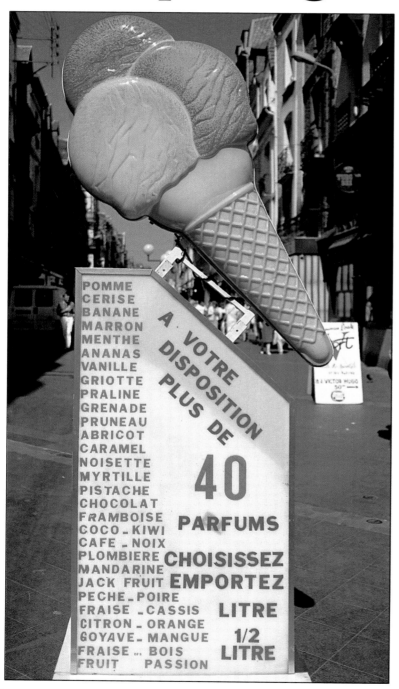

Until about 100 years ago, many people could not read. Signs were put outside shops to help people recognize them. There is no mistaking what this shop sells!

The old barber's pole is still seen in some places. At one time, **barbers** were also often doctors. The red and white stripes of the pole stood for the blood and bandages.

Activity

Design and paint a sign for a new pet shop. Do not use any words; use only pictures and symbols.

Coats of arms

When the **knights** of old wore their **armor**, it was difficult to tell one person from another. So each knight painted a different design on his shield. The same pattern was sewn on his coat.

These "coats of arms" belonged to only one family and were handed down from father to son.

CITY OF LONDON

Towns, counties, and even countries have coats of arms too.

Each state has its own coat of arms. It is called a state seal. Sometimes this can give you clues to what might be found in or near the place.

NEW BERN
17 10
NORTH CAROLINA

Activity

Design a personal coat of arms with symbols of people and things that are important to you.

Flags

Each country in the world has its own flag. A flag can tell you something about a country.

The British flag is called the Union Jack. It is made up of three flags. What three flags are included in it?

The flag of the United States of America is called the Stars and Stripes. There is a star to stand for each state.

Pirates used to fly a flag called *The Jolly Roger*. The skull and cross-bones was meant to frighten the people they attacked. It was a sign that said you were about to be robbed.

Badges

People wear all kinds of badges. They often have a special design or **logo** on them.

Badges can give different messages. They can be worn just for fun, or they might have a more serious message. People often wear badges to show that they like or agree with something.

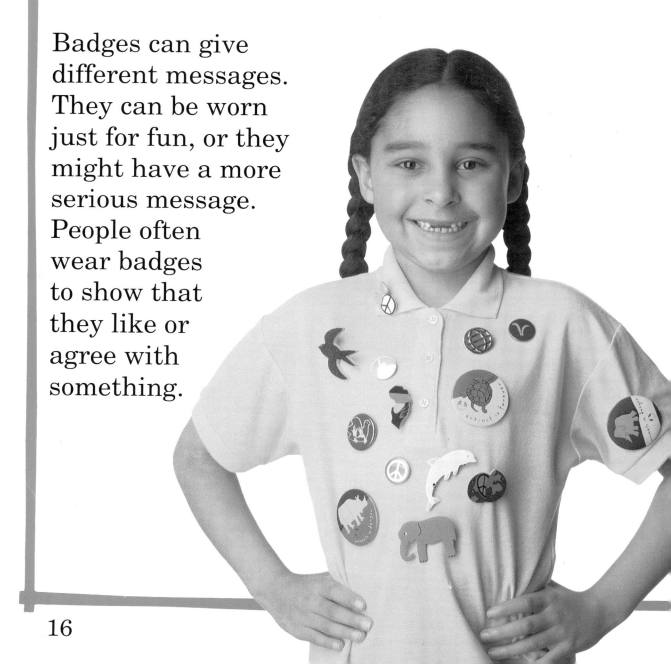

Other badges show that someone has achieved something. These girls are wearing special medals to show that their soccer team has won a competition.

Advertising signs

Signs and symbols are often used in **advertising**. Companies make up simple symbols or logos that help people recognize things they make.

Advertising logos are carefully designed to make you want to buy something. They might make the thing they are advertising seem exciting or delicious.

Activity

Make a collection of different logos. Which do you think are the best? Why?

Picture signs

If you have a lot of information, signs can be used to make things clearer. You can use simple pictures called **pictograms** to make a chart. These children asked their friends to name their favorite fruit.

They made a pictogram chart to show clearly what they found out. Each fruit symbol stands for two children who like that fruit best. Eight children liked apples best. If an odd number of children liked apples, how could this be shown?

Activity

Make a pictogram chart for the pets your friends own, or would most like to own.

21

Sounds interesting!

Before telephones or radios were invented, people found many ways to send information over long distances. In some parts of the world, trees and drums were used to beat out messages. They could be heard by other people far away.

Muslims are called to prayer by a **muezzin** who sings out from the **Mosque**. In Europe, church bells are sometimes rung to warn, call, or tell people things.

A siren heard in the street is a sign that an ambulance, police car, or fire engine is coming. What sounds at home or in school send messages?

Fire signals

At night, bonfires lit on hills can be seen from a long way off. In the past, these beacons were used to send important messages. These were usually warnings about approaching armies.

The first lighthouses were simply bonfires lit on the cliff tops. They warned ships to keep away from dangerous rocks. Now powerful electric lights are used instead.

Sign language

Instead of talking, many people who cannot hear learn a sign language.

These two men are in a **travel agent's** office. They are discussing vacations by making signs and **gestures** with their hands, arms, and faces.

Think of ways to send messages to a friend just by using signs.

This boy is being taught how to use sign language. Deaf people can also learn to lipread. By watching people's lips when they are talking, they can tell what is being said.

Map symbols

Symbols on maps are used to give information about a place.

These children are designing map symbols. A few little trees might stand for a forest. A cross stands for a church. You can find out what a symbol means by looking at the **key**.

The key for this map hasn't been finished. It should say what each symbol means. What do you think should be written next to each symbol?

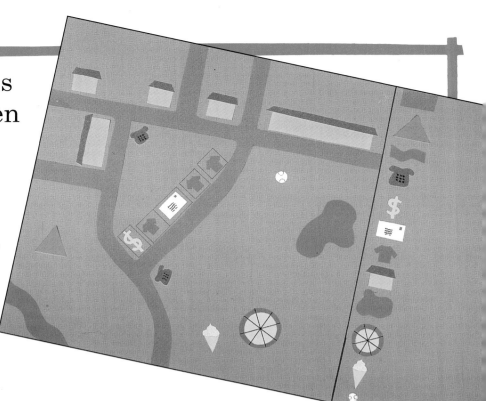

Activity

Draw an alien's map for a piece of land on another planet. Make up your own symbols and explain their meanings in a key.

Glossary

Advertising Ways of telling people about something, usually to help sell it.

Armor Special suits made out of metal that soldiers used to wear to protect themselves in battle.

Barbers People who cut hair.

Campsite A place where people camp in tents, caravans, or trailers.

Gestures Movements of the body that tell you something.

Key A chart that explains what the symbols on a map mean.

Knights Soldiers who were given an important place in an army by a king or queen.

Logo A special symbol that makes you think of one product or organization.

Mosque A place where Muslims go to pray.

Muezzin A man who reminds Muslims when it is time to pray by calling from the Mosque.

Muslims People who believe in the religion of Islam.

Pictogram A picture symbol used instead of writing. A chart using such symbols.

Recycling The way waste materials are changed into something that can be used again.

Travel Agent Someone whom you pay to organize your travel and vacations.

Books to read

Greene, Laura and Eva Barash Dicker. *Sign Language*. First Books. New York: Franklin Watts, 1981.

Kalman, Bobbie. *How We Communicate*. New York: Crabtree Publishing Co., 1986.

Nelson, Nigel. *Body Talk*. Nonverbal Communications. New York: Thomson Learning, 1993.

Schneider, D. Douglas. *Symbolically Speaking*. Eugene, OR: World Peace Univ., 1987.

Wake, Susan. *Advertising*. Ada, OK: Garrett Educational Corp., 1991.

Index